MAKING FRIENDS WITH MY EMOTIONS

IT'S OK TO BE FRUSTRATED

THERESA EMMINIZER

PowerKiDS press

Published in 2025 by The Rosen Publishing Group, Inc.
2544 Clinton Street, Buffalo, NY 14224

First Edition

Editor: Theresa Emminizer
Book Design: Michael Flynn

Photo Credits: Cover, p. 1 Brastock/Shutterstock.com; (series background) Sergei Mishchenko/Shutterstock.com; p. 5 imtmphoto/Shutterstock.com; p. 7 wavebreakmedia/Shutterstock.com; p. 9 chaythawin/Shutterstock.com; p. 11 Prostock-studio/Shutterstock.com; p. 13 Cookie Studio/Shutterstock.com; p. 15 Marius Pirvu/Shutterstock.com; p. 17 Flotsam/Shutterstock.com; p. 19 fizkes/Shutterstock.com; p. 21 Bricolage/Shutterstock.com.

Library of Congress Cataloging-in-Publication Data

Names: Emminizer, Theresa, author.
Title: It's ok to be frustrated / Theresa Emminizer.
Description: [Buffalo] : PowerKids Press, [2025] | Series: Making friends with my emotions | Includes bibliographical references and index. |
Audience: Grades K-1
Identifiers: LCCN 2023054216 (print) | LCCN 2023054217 (ebook) | ISBN 9781499445053 (library binding) | ISBN 9781499445046 (paperback) | ISBN 9781499445060 (ebook)
Subjects: LCSH: Frustration in children–Juvenile literature. |
Frustration–Juvenile literature.
Classification: LCC BF723.F7 E46 2025 (print) | LCC BF723.F7 (ebook) |
DDC 155.4/1247-dc23/eng/20231218
LC record available at https://lccn.loc.gov/2023054216
LC ebook record available at https://lccn.loc.gov/2023054217

Manufactured in the United States of America

Some of the images in this book illustrate individuals who are models. The depictions do not imply actual situations or events.

CPSIA Compliance Information: Batch #CSPK25. For Further Information contact Rosen Publishing at 1-800-237-9932.

CONTENTS

Feeling Frustrated

Frustration is something we feel when things don't go the way we want them to. What does it feel like to be frustrated? Your face might feel hot. Your **jaw** might feel tight. Feeling frustrated isn't fun. But there are ways to **cope**.

Why Does It Happen?

There are lots of different reasons you might feel frustrated. Maybe you really want to sleep over at a friend's house but your mom says no. Maybe you've been working really hard on a drawing but it doesn't turn out the way you pictured it.

It's OK!

Whatever the reason is, big or small, it's OK to feel frustrated! Frustration is a natural part of life. You don't have to feel bad about getting frustrated or hide it away. It's what you do with your frustration that matters most.

Losing Control

Jamila was frustrated. No matter how hard she tried, she just couldn't understand math. Finally, she couldn't take it anymore. Jamila threw her books on the floor. She gave an angry shout! She stomped out of the classroom without looking back.

Find Your Calm

When we're frustrated, it can be hard to control our body. We may want to throw things. We may even want to yell or hit someone. It's important to find ways to calm, or quiet, yourself so you don't do something you wish you hadn't.

Take a Beat

Steve was learning to drum. Practicing was hard! He could feel the frustration rushing through his body. When that happened, his teacher said: "Take a beat." Steve stopped. He took a deep breath. He felt his body **relax** a little bit. He felt ready to try again.

Ways to Cope

Here are some helpful ways to work through frustration:

- Put your hands together. Push and let go.
- Breathe in through your nose. Count to four. Breathe out through your mouth. Count to four.
- Write down what's bothering you. Rip up the paper.

You're Not Alone

Everybody in the world feels frustrated sometimes. Tell someone you trust about how you're feeling! If you feel out of control, ask for help. Just talking about your frustration can make you feel much better. If you don't feel like talking, write, draw, or sing about it.

Making Friends with Frustration

Frustration doesn't feel good. But it's part of life. When you're frustrated, it helps to know it won't last forever. Remember, feelings come and feelings go. Take a breath. Feel your feet on the ground. Press your hands together. It's OK to be frustrated!

GLOSSARY

cope: Dealing with or working through your feelings.

jaw: The upper and lower bones of your mouth.

relax: To become calm or less tense.

FOR MORE INFORMATION

BOOKS

Bromage, Fran. *I Can: I Can Feel.* New York, NY: Windmill Books, 2023.

McAneney, Caitie. *I Use Mindfulness to Cope.* New York, NY: PowerKids Press, 2023.

WEBSITES

Kids Health
kidshealth.org/en/kids/anger.html
Learn more about anger and how to handle it.

PBS Kids
pbskids.org/learn/lifes-little-lessons/mad-feelings/
Learn more ways to cope with hard feelings.

INDEX